T0070107

HIGHWAY 10/20

MICHAEL ANTHONY

authorHOUSE®

AuthorHouse™
1663 Liberty Drive
Bloomington, IN 47403
www.authorhouse.com
Phone: 1 (800) 839-8640

NKJV
Scripture quotations marked NKJV are taken from the New King James Version. Copyright © 1982 by Thomas Nelson, Inc. Used by permission. All rights reserved.

Published by AuthorHouse   01/25/2016

ISBN: 978-1-5049-7539-1 (sc)
ISBN: 978-1-5049-7538-4 (e)

Print information available on the last page.

This book is printed on acid-free paper.

BEFORE YOU BEGIN....

J ERRY THE PARAKEET NEVER saw it coming. One second he was perched peacefully in his cage. The next thing he was sucked up, washed up, and blown over.

The problem began when Jerry's owner decided to clean Jerry's cage with a vacuum cleaner. She removed the attachments from the end of the hose and stuck it in the cage. The phone rang and she turned to answer it. She'd barely said "hello" when "sssopp!" Jerry got sucked in.

The bird owner gasped, put down the phone, and turned of the vacuum, and opened the bag. There was Jerry—still alive, but stunned.

Since the bird was covered in dust and soot, she grabbed him and rushed him to the bathroom, turned on the faucet, and held Jerry under the running water. Then, what any compassionate bird owner would do...she reached for the hair dryer and blasted the pet with hot air. Poor Jerry never knew what hit him.

A few days after the trauma, the reporter who initially written about the event contacted Jerry's owner to see how Jerry was recovering. "Well," she replied, "Jerry doesn't sing much anymore—he just sits and stares."

It's hard not to see why. Sucked in, washed up, and blown over…that's enough to steal the song from the stoutest heart.

Can you relate to Jerry? Most of can. One minute you're seated with a song on your lip, and then…The pink slip comes. The rejection letter comes. The doctor calls. The divorce papers are delivered. The check bounces. The policeman knocks on the door.

Sssopp! You're sucked in to a black cavern of doubts, doused with cold water of reality, and stung with hot air of empty promises.

The life that had been so calm is now so stormy. You're hailstormed by demands. Assailed by doubts. Pummeled by questions. And somewhere in the trauma, you lose your joy. Somewhere in the storm, you lose your song.

Ever found yourself in the storm of life? If so, if Jerry's story is your story, then I'm glad you picked up this book. I wrote it with you in mind. Driving down the highway your mind can begin to imagine what life is, what it could have been, and what it should be.

The highway of life is the mirror of the highway of the country. Storms come. They come quickly. They pounce ferociously. If you are in one, then you know what I mean. If you are not in one today, you knew as well as I—one may be in tomorrow's forecast.

My prayer is that this book will leave you better prepared. My prayer is that you will find some word, some story, some verse, or some thought that will convince you that He is very near. I pray that as you read you will be reminded that the same voice that stilled the rage on the Sea of Galilee can still the storm in your world.

Read on, friend, and be assured—He is closer than you have ever dreamed!!

DOUBTSTORMS

There are snowstorms. There are hailstorms. There are rainstorms. And there are doubt storms. Every so often a doubt storm rolls into my life, bringing with it a flurry of questions and gale-forced winds of fear. And, soon after it comes, a light shines through it.

Sometimes the storm comes after the evening news. Some nights I wonder why I watch it. Some nights it's just too much. From the steps of the Supreme Court to the steppes of South Africa, the news is usually gloomy....thirty minutes of bite-sized tragedies. A handsome man with a nice suit with a warm voice gives bad news. They call him the anchorman. Good title. One needs an anchorman in today's tempestuous waters.

Sometimes I wonder, How can our world get so chaotic? Sometimes the storm comes when I am at work. Story after story of homes that won't heal and hearts that won't melt. Always more hunger than food. More needs than money. More questions than answers. A prayer on my lips, I do my best to say something that will convince a stranger that an unseen God still hears. And I sometimes wonder why so many hearts have to hurt.

Do you ever get doubt storms? Some of you don't, I've talked to you. Some of you have "Davidish" optimism that defies any Goliath. I used to think you were naïve at best and phony at worst. I don't think that anymore.

I think you are gifted. You are gifted with faith. You can see the rainbow before the clouds part. If you have this gift I won't say anything you want to hear. But others of you wonder....

You wonder what others know that you don't. You wonder if you are blind or if they are. You wonder why some proclaim "Eureka" before the gold is found. You wonder why some shout "Land ho" before the fog has cleared. You wonder how some believe so confidently while you believe so reluctantly.

As a result, you are a bit uncomfortable on the padded pew of unbelief. Your Bible hero is Thomas. Your middle name is Caution. Your queries are the bane of every Sunday school teacher.

"If God is so good, why do I sometimes feel so bad?"

"If His message is so clear, why do I get so confused?"

"If the Father is in control, why do good people have gut-wrenching problems?"

You wonder if it is a blessing or a curse to have a mind that never rests. But you would rather be a cynic than a hypocrite, so continue to pray with one eye open and wonder:

About starving children

About power of prayer

About depths of grace

About Christians in cancer wards

About who you are to ask such a question.

Tough questions. Throw-in-the-towel questions. Questions that the disciples must have asked in the storm. All they could see was black skies as the bounced in the battered boat. Swirling clouds. Wind-driven white caps. Pessimism that buried the coastline. Gloom that swamped the bow. What could have been a pleasant trip became a white-knuckled ride through the sea of fear.

Their question-What hope do we have in surviving a stormy night?

Doubt storms: turbulent days when the enemy is too big, the task is too great, the future too bleak, and the answers too few.

Every so often a storm will come, and I'll look up into the blackening sky and say, "God, a little light, please?" The light came for the disciples. A figure came to them walking on the water. It wasn't what they expected. Perhaps they were looking for angels to descend or heaven to open. Maybe they were listening for a divine proclamation to still the storm. We don't know what they were looking for. But one thing is for sure, they weren't looking for Jesus to come walking on water.

"It's a ghost,' they cried out in fear." And since Jesus came in a way they didn't expect, they almost missed seeing the answer to their prayers.

And unless we look and listen closely, we risk making the same mistake. God's light in our dark nights is as numerous as the stars, if only we'll look for them.

Can I share a couple of lights that have illuminated my world recently?

Light number one came from the intensive care ward where my mother had been a couple of weeks ago. I walked into the wrong room and I had the privilege to speak to who I can say is a friend.

"We will celebrate forty-four years tomorrow," Jack said, feeding his wife. She was bald. Her eyes were sunken, and her speech was slurred. She looked strait ahead, only opening her mouth when he brought the fork near. He wiped her cheek. He wiped his brow.

"She has been sick for five years," he told me. "She can't walk. She can't take care of herself. She can't even feed herself, but I love her. And," he spoke louder where she could hear, "we are going to beat this thing, aren't we, Honey?"

He fed her a few bites and spoke again, "We don't have insurance. When I could afford it, I thought I wouldn't need it. Now I owe this hospital more than $50,000." He was quiet for a few moments while he gave her a drink. Then he continued. "But they don't pester me. They know I can't pay, but they admitted us with no questions asked. The doctors treat us like we are the best-paying patients. Who would've imagined such kindness?"

I had to agree with him. Who would have imagined such kindness? In a thorny world of high-tech, expensive, often criticized health care, it was reassuring to find professionals who would serve two who had nothing to give in return.

Jack thanked me for listening, and I thanked God that once again sinew of light reminded me of the sun behind the clouds.

A few days later, another light.

David Gerrard is the quarterback of the Jacksonville Jaguars. I don't know him personally. Gerrard recently spent the afternoon at a local men's store, signing autographs. He was scheduled to spend two hours, but ended up spending three. Pencil-and-pad-toting kids besieged the place, asking him questions and shaking his hand.

When he was able to slip out, he climbed into his car, only to notice a touching sight. A late-arriving youngster peddled up, jumped off his bike, and ran to the window to see if the quarterback was still at the store. When he saw he wasn't, he turned slowly and sadly, walked over to his bike and began to ride off.

David Gerrard turned off the ignition, climbed out of his car, and walked over to the boy. They chatted a few minutes, went next door, and sat down at a table, and had a soft drink.

No reporters were near. No cameras were on. As far as these two knew, noone knew. I'm sure David Gerrard had other things to do that afternoon. No doubt he had other appointments to keep. But it's doubtful that anything he might have done that afternoon was more important than what he did.

In a world of big-bucked, high-glossed professional sports, it did me good to hear of one player is a player at heart. Hearing what he did was enough to blow away any lingering clouds of doubt and to leave me warmed by God's light…..his gentle light.

Gentle lights. God's solutions for doubt storms. Gold-flecked glows that amber hope into blackness. Not thunderbolts. Not explosions of light. Just gentle lights.

A hospital choosing compassion. A celebrity choosing kindness.

Visible evidence of the invisible hand. Soft reminders that optimism is not just for fools. Funny. None of the events were "religious." None of the encounters occurred in a ceremony or a church service. None will make the six o'clock news.

But such is the case with gentle lights.

When the disciples saw Jesus in the middle of their stormy night, they called him a ghost. A phantom. A hallucination. To them, the glow was anything but God.

When we see gentle lights in the horizon, we often have the same reaction. We dismiss occasional kindness as apparitions, accidents, or anomalies. Anything but God.

"When Jesus comes," the disciples in the boat may have thought, "he'll split the sky. The sea will be calm. The clouds will disperse."

"When God comes," we doubters think, "all pain will flee. Life will be tranquil. No questions will remain." And because we look for the bonfire, we miss the candle. Because we listen for the shout, we miss the whisper.

But it is in the burnished candles that God comes, and through whispered promises he speaks: "When you doubt, look around; I am closer than u think.

SEEING GOD THROUGH A SHATTERED GLASS

There is a window in your heart through which you can see God. Once upon a time that window was clear. Your view of God was crisp. You could see God vividly as you could see a gentle valley or hillside. The glass was clean, the pane unbroken.

You knew God. You knew how he worked. You knew what he wanted you to do. No surprises. Nothing unexpected. You knew that God had a will, and you continually discovered what it was. Then, suddenly, the window cracked. A pebble broke the window. A pebble of pain.

Perhaps the stone struck when you were child and a parent left home – forever. Maybe the rock hit in adolescence when your heart was broken. Maybe the rock hit in adolescence when your heart was broken. Maybe you made it into adulthood before the window was cracked. But then the pebble came.

Was it a phone call? "We have your daughter at the station you better come down." Was it a letter on the kitchen table? "I've left. Don't try to reach me. Don't try to call me.

It's over. I just don't love you anymore." Was it a diagnosis from the doctor? "I'm afraid our news is not very good. Was it a telegram? "We regret to inform you that your son is missing in action."

Whatever the pebble's form, the result was the same – a shattered window. The pebble missile into the pane and shattered it. The crashed echoed through the halls of your heart. Cracks shot out from the point of impact, creating a spider web of fragmented pieces.

And suddenly God was not so easy to see. The view that had been so crisp had changed. You turned to see God, and his figure was distorted. It was hard to see him through the pain. It was hard to see him through the fragments of hurt.

You were puzzled. "God wouldn't allow something like that to happen, would he? Tragedy and travesty weren't out agenda of the one you had seen, were they? Had you been fooled? Had you been blind?

The moment the pebble struck, the glass became a reference point for you. From then on, there was life before the pain and life after the pain. Before the pain, the view was clear, God seemed so near. After your pain, well he was hard to see. He seemed a bit distant......harder to perceive. Your pain distorted your view – not eclipsed it, but distorted it.

Maybe these words don't describe your situation. There are some people who never have to redefine or refocus their view of God. Most of us do.

Most of us have a way of completing this sentence: "If God were God, the............" Call it an agenda, a divine job description. Each of us has an unspoken, yet definitive, expectation of what God should do. "If God is God, then....."

- There will be no financial collapse in my family.
- My children will never be buried before me.
- People will treat me fairly.
- This church will never divide.
- My prayer will be answered.

These are not articles of criteria. They are not written down or notarized. But they are real. They define the expectations we have of God. And when pain comes into our world – when the careening pebble splinters the window of our hearts – the expectations go unmet and doubts may begin to surface.

We look for God, but can't find him. Fragmented glass hinders our vision. He is enlarged through this piece and reduced through that one. Lines jigsaw their way across his face. Large sections of shattered glass opaque the view.

And now you aren't quite sure of what you see.

The disciples weren't sure what they saw, either. Jesus failed to meet their expectations. The day Jesus fed the five thousand men he didn't do what they wanted him to do.

The twelve returned from their mission followed by an army. They finished their training. They recruited the soldiers. They were ready for battle. They expected Jesus to let the crowds crown him as King and attack the city of Herod. They expected battle plans.....strategies.....and new era for Israel.

What did the get? Just the opposite. Instead of weapons, they got ears. Rather than getting sent to fight, they were sent to float. The crowds were sent away. Jesus walked away.

And they were left on the water with a storm brewing in the sky.

What kind of Messiah would do this?

Note carefully the sequence of the stormy evening as Matthew records it.

Immediately Jesus made the disciples get into the boat and go on ahead of him to the other side, while he dismissed the crowd. After he had dismissed them, he went up to the mountainside by himself to pray. When evening came, he was their alone, but the boat was already a considerably distance from land, buffeted by the waves because the wind was against it.

Matthew is specific about the order of events. Jesus went the disciples to the boat. Then he dismissed the crowds ascended a mountainside. It was evening, probably around 6:00 p.m. The storm struck immediately. The sun had scarce set before typhoon – like winds began to roar.

Note Jesus sent the disciples into the storm alone. Even as he was ascending the mountainside, he could feel and hear the gate's force. Jesus was not ignorant of the storm. He was aware a torrent was coming that would carpet-bomb the sea's surface. But he didn't turn around. The disciples were left to face the storm....alone.

The greatest storm that night was not in the sky; it was in the disciples hearts. The greatest fear was not from seeing the storm-driven waves; it came from seeing the back of their leader as he left them to face the night with only questions as companions.

It was this fury that the disciples were facing that night. Imagine the incredible strain of bouncing from wave to wave in a tiny fishing vessel. One hour would weary you. Two hours would exhaust you.

Surely Jesus will help us, they thought. They'd seen him still storms like this before. On this same sea, they had awaken him during a storm, and he had commanded the sky silent. They'd seen him quiet the winds and soothe the waves. Surely he will come off the mountain.

But he doesn't. Their arms begin to ache from rowing. Still no sign of Jesus. Three hours. 4 hours. The winds rage. The boat bounces. Still no Jesus. Midnight comes. Their eyes search for God – in vain.

By now the disciples have been on the sea for as long as six hours.

All this time they have fought the storm and sought the Master. And, so far, the storm is winning. And the Master is nowhere to be found.

"Where is he?" cried one. "Has he forgotten us?" Yelled another. "He has fed thousands of others strangers and get leaves us to die?" Muttered a third.

The gospel of Mark adds compelling insight into the disciples attitude. "They had not understood about the loaves; their hearts were hardened."

What does Mark mean? Simply this. The disciples were mad. They began the evening in a huff. Their hearts were hardened toward Jesus because he fed the multitude. Their preference, remember, had been to "send the crowds away." And Jesus told them to feed the people. But they wouldn't try. They said it couldn't be done. They told Jesus to let the people take care of themselves.

Also, keep in mind that the disciples had just spent some time on center stage. They'd tasted stardom. They were celebrities. They had rallied crowds. They had recruited an army. They were, no doubt, pretty proud of themselves. With chests a bit puffy and heads a bit swollen, they'd told Jesus, "Just send them away."

Jesus didn't. Instead he chose to bypass the reluctant disciples and use the faith of an anonymous boy. What the disciples said couldn't be done was done – in spite of them not through them.

They pouted. They sulked. Rather than being amazed at the miracle, they became mad at the Master. After all, the felt foolish passing out the very bread they said could not be made. Add to that Jesus' commend go to the boat when they wanted to go to battle, and it's easier to understand and see why these guys are burning!

"Now what is Jesus up to, leaving us out on sea on a night like this?"

It's 1:00 a.m., no Jesus. It's 2:00 a.m., no Jesus. Peter, Andrew, James, and John have seen storms like this. They are fishermen; the sea is their life. They know the havoc the gale-force winds can wreak. They've seen the splintered hulls float to shore. They've attended the funerals. They know, better than anyone, that this night could be their last. "Why doesn't he come?" they sputter.

Finally he does. "During the fourth watch at the night [3:00 am to 6:00 am] Jesus went out to them, walking on the lake.

Jesus came. He finally came. But between verse 24 – being buffeted by the waves – and verse 25 – when Jesus appeared – a thousand questions are asked.

Questions you have probably asked, too. Perhaps you know the angst of being suspended between verses 24 and

25. Maybe you are riding a storm, searching the coastline for a light, a glimmer of hope. You know that Jesus knows what you are going through. You know he's aware of your storm. But as hard as you look to find him, you can't see him. Maybe your heart, like the disciples' hearts, has been gardened by unmet expectations. Your pleadings for help are salted with angry questions. Stress attacks your nerves. Storms attack your faith. Stress interrupts. Storms destroy. Stress comes like a siren. Storms come like a missile. Stress clouds the day. Storms usher in the night.

The question of stress is, "How can I cope?" The question of storm is, "Where is God and why would he do this?"

These pages are for you if the pebble of pain has struck the window of your heart, if you've known the horror of looking for Gods face and seeing only his back as he ascends a mountainside.

I hope this is a message for those who know the anxiety of searching for God in a storm.

The message? When you can't see him, trust him. The figure you see is not a ghost. The voice you hear is not the wind. Jesus is closer than you've ever dreamed.

BEHIND THE SHOWER CURTAIN

I'm going to have to install a computer in my shower. That's where I have my best thoughts. I had a great one today. I was mulling over a recent conversation I had with a disenchanted Christian brother. He was upset with me. Seems he'd heard I was pretty open about who I fellowship with. He'd heard of some words I spoke: "If God calls a person his child, shouldn't I call him my brother?" And, "If God accepts others with their errors and misinterpretations, shouldn't we?"

He didn't like that. "Carrying it a bit too far," he told me. Fences are necessary," he explained. Scriptures are clear on such matters." He read me a few and then urged me to be careful to whom I give grace. "I don't give it," I assured. "I only spotlight where God already has." It didn't seem to satisfy him. I offered to bow out of confrontation, but he softened up after that. That is why I was thinking about him in the shower. And that is why I need a waterproof computer. I had a great thought. A why-didn't-I-think-to-say-that? Insight.

I hope to see him today. If the subject resurfaces, I'll say it. But in case it doesn't, I'll say it to you. (It's too good to waste.) Just one sentence:

I've never been surprised by God's judgment, but I'm still stunned by His grace.

God's judgment has never been a problem for me. In fact, it always seems right. Lightning bolts on Sodom. Fire on Gomorrah. *Good job, God.* Egyptians swallowed up in the Red Sea. *They had it coming.* Forty years of wondering to loosen the stiff necks of the Israelites? *I would have done it myself.* Ananias and Sapphira? *You bet.* Discipline is easy for me to swallow. Logical to assimilate. Manageable and appropriate. But God's grace? Anything but. Examples? How much time do you have?

David the Psalmist becomes David the voyeur, but by God's grace becomes David the Psalmist again. Peter denied Christ before he preached the Christ. Zacchaeus the crook. The cleanest part of his life was the money he laundered. But Jesus still had time for him. The thief on the cross: hell bent and hung out to die one minute, heaven-bound and smiling the next.

Story after story. Prayer after prayer. Surprise after surprise.

Seems that God is looking more for ways to get us home than for ways to keep us out. I challenge you to find on soul that came to God seeking grace and did not find it. Search the pages. Read the stories. Envision the encounters. Find one person who came seeking a second chance and left with a stern lecture. I dare you search. You won't find it.

You will find a strayed sheep on the other side of the creek. He's lost. He knows it. He's stuck and embarrassed. What will the other sheep say?

You will find a shepherd who finds him. *Oh boy. Duck down. Put hooves over the eyes. The belt is about to fly.* But the belt is never felt. Just hands. Large open hands reaching under his body and lifting the sheep up, up, up until he's place on the shepherd's shoulders. He's carried back to the flock and given a party! "Cut the grass and comb the wool," he announces. "We are going to have a celebration!" The other sheep shake their heads in disbelief. Just like we will. At our party. When we get home. When we watch the Shepherd shoulder into our mist one unlikely soul after another.

Seems to me God gives a lot more grace than we'd ever imagine. We could do the same.

I'm not watering down the truth or compromising the gospel. But if a fellow with a pure heart calls God *Father,* can't I call the same man *Brother?* If God does not make doctrinal perfection a requirement for family membership, should I?

And if we never agree, can't we agree to disagree? If God can tolerate my mistakes, can't I tolerate the mistakes of others? If God can overlook my errors, can't I overlook the errors of others? If God allows me with my foibles and failures to call Him *Father,* shouldn't I extend the same grace to others?

For one things for sure. When we get to heaven, we'll be surprised at some of the folks we will see. And some of them will be surprised when they see us.

GABRIEL'S QUESTIONS

GABRIEL MUST HAVE scratched his head at this one. He wasn't one to question his God-given missions. Sending fire and dividing seas were all in an eternity's work for this angel. When God sent Gabriel went.

And when word got out that God was to become man, Gabriel was enthused. He could envision the moment:

The Messiah in a blazing chariot.

The king descending on a fiery cloud.

An explosion of light from where the Messiah would emerge.

That's what he expected. What he never expected, however, is what he got: a slip of paper with a Nazarene address. "God will become a baby," it read. "Tell the mother to name the child Jesus. And tell her not to be afraid."

Gabriel was not one to question, but this time he had to wonder.

God will become a baby? Gabriel had seen babies before. He had been platoon leader on the bulrush operation. He remembered what little Moses looked like.

That's ok for humans, he thought to himself. *But God?*

The heavens can't contain him; how could a body? Besides have you seen what comes out of those babies? Hardly befitting for the Creator of the universe. Babies must be carried and fed, bounced and bathed. To imagine some mother burping God on her shoulder—why, that was beyond even what an angel could imagine.

And what of this name—what was it—*Jesus?* Such a common name. There's a Jesus an every cul-de-sac. Come on, even *Gabriel* has more punch than *Jesus.* Call the baby *Eminence* or *Majesty* or *Heaven-sent.* Anything but *Jesus.*

So Gabriel scratched his head. What happen to the good ol' days? The Sodom and Gomorrah stuff. Flooding the globe. Flaming swords. That's the action he liked.

But Gabriel had his orders. Take the message to Mary. *Must be a special girl,* he assumed as he traveled. But Gabriel was in for another shock. One peek told him Mary was no queen. The mother-to-be of God was not regal. She was a Jewish peasant who'd barely out grown her acne and had a crush on a guy name Joe.

And speaking of Joe-what does this fellow know? Might as well be a weaver in Spain or a cobbler in Greece. He's a carpenter. Look at him over there, sawdust on his beard and nail apron around his waist. You're telling me that God is going to have dinner every night with him? You're telling me that the source of wisdom is going to be calling this guy "*Dad*"? You're telling me that this laborer is going to be charged with giving food to God?

What if he gets laid off?

What if he gets cranky?

What if he decides to runoff with a pretty young girl from down the street? Then where will we be?

It was all Gabriel could do to keep from turning back. "This is a peculiar idea you have, God," he must have muttered to himself.

Are God's guardians given such musings?

Are we? Are we still stunned by God's coming? Still staggered by the event? Does Christmas still spawn the same speechless wonder it did two thousand years ago?

I've been asking that question lately—to myself. As I write, Christmas is only a few days away and something just happened that has me concerned that the pace of the holidays may be overshadowing the purpose of the holidays.

I saw a manger in the mall. Correct that. I *barely* saw a manger in the mall. I almost didn't see it. I was in a hurry. Guest coming. Santa dropping in. Presents to be purchased.

The crush of the things was so great that the crèche of Christ was almost ignored. I nearly missed it. Had it not been for a child and his father, I would have.

But out of the corner of my eye, I saw them. The little boy, three, maybe four years old, in jeans and high—tops staring at the manger's infant. The father, in baseball hat and work clothes, looking over his son's shoulder, gesturing first at Joseph, then Mary, then the baby. He was telling the little fellow the story.

And oh, the twinkle in the boy's eyes. The wonder on his little face. He didn't speak. He just listened. And I didn't move. I just watched. What questions were filling the little boy's head? Could they have been the same as Gabriel's? What sparked the amazement on his face? Was it the magic?

And why is it out of a hundred or so of God's children only two paused to consider his son? What is this December demon that steals our eyes and stills our tongues? Isn't this the season to pause and pose Gabriel's questions?

The tragedy is not that we can't answer them, but that we are too busy to ask them. Only heaven knows how long Gabriel fluttered unseen above Mary before he took a breath and broke the news. But he did. He told her the name. He told her the plan. He told her not to be afraid. And when he announced, "With God nothing is impossible!" he said it as much for himself as for her.

For even though he couldn't answer the questions, he knew who could, and that was enough. And even though we can't answer them all, taking the time to ask a few would be a good start.

GRACE AND GROCERIES

Seems a fellow is doing some shopping at a commissary on a military base. Doesn't need much, just some coffee and a loaf of bread. He is standing in line at the checkout stand. Behind him is a woman with a full cart. Her basket overflows with groceries, clothing, and a VCR.

At his turn he steps up to the register. The clerk invites him to draw a piece of paper out of the fishbowl. "If you pull out the correct slip, then all your groceries are free," the clerk explains.

"How many 'correct slips' are there?" asks the buyer.

"Only one."

The bowl is full so the chances are slim, but the fellow tries anyway, and wouldn't you know it, he gets the winning ticket! What a surprise. But then he realizes that he is only getting coffee and bread. What a waste.

But this fellow is quick. He turns to the lady behind him--the one with the mountain of stuff—and proclaims, "Well, what do you know, Honey? We won! We don't have to pay a penny."

She stares at him. He winks at her. And somehow she has the wherewithal to play along. She steps up besides him. Puts her arm in his and smiles. For a moment they stand side-by-side, wedded by good fortune. In the parking lot she consummates the temporary union with a kiss and a hug and goes on her way with a grand story to tell her friends.

I know, I know. What they did was a bit shady. He shouldn't have lied and she shouldn't have pretended. But that taken to account, it's still a nice story.

A story not too distant from our own. We, too, have been graced with a surprise. Even more than that of the lady. For though her debt was high, she could pay it. We can't begin to pay ours.

We, like the woman, have been given a gift. Not just for a moment, but for eternity. And not just for groceries, but for the feast. Don't we have a grand story to tell our friends?

MAXIMS

HERE'S A TOAST to the simple sentence. Here is a salute to the one-liners. Join me in applauding the delete key and the eraser.

May they feast on the trimmings of the writer's table. I believe in brevity. Cut the fat and keep the fact. Give us words to chew on, not words to wade through. Thoughts that spark, not lines that drag. More periods. Fewer commas.

Distill it.

Barebone it.

Bare-knuckle it.

Concise (but not cute). Clear (but not shallow). Vivid (but not detailed). That's good writing. That's good reading. But that's hard work!

But, it's what we like. We appreciate the chef who cuts the gristle before he serves the steak. We salute the communicator who does the same.

Ahhh, brevity. An art apparently unheeded in the realms of insurance brochures and some-assembly-bicycle manuals.

We learn brevity from Jesus. His greatest sermon can be read in eight minutes (Matthew 5-7). His best known story can be read in ninety seconds (Luke 15:11-32). He summarized prayer in five phrases (Matt 6:9-13). He silenced accusers with one challenge (John 8:7). He rescued a soul with one sentence (Luke 23:43). He summarized the Law with three verses (Mark 12:29-31), and he reduced all his teachings to one command (John 15:12).

He made his point and went home.

We preachers would do well to imitate. (What's that old line? "Our speaker today needs no introduction, but he could use a conclusion.")

I believe in brevity. I believe that you, the reader, entrust me, the writer, with your most valued commodity—your time. I shouldn't take more than my share. For that reason, I love the short sentence. Big—time game it is. Hiding in the jungle of circular construction and six syllable canyons. As I write, I hunt. And when I find, I shoot. Then I drag the treasure out from the trees and marvel.

Not all of my prey make their way into the chapters. So what becomes of them? I save them. But I can't keep them to myself. So, may I invite you to see my trophy case? What follows are cuts from this book and a couple of others. Keep the ones you like. Forgive the ones you don't. Share them when you can. But if you do; keep it brief.

Pray all the time. If necessary, use words.
Sacrilege is to feel guilty for sins forgiven.
God forgets the past. Imitate him.
Greed I've often regretted. Generosity—never.
Never miss an opportunity to read a child a story.
Pursue forgiveness, not innocence.
Be double kind to people who bring your food or park your car.
In buying a gift for your wife, practicality can be more expensive than extravagance.

Don't ask God to do what you want. Ask God to do what is right.

Nails didn't hold God to the cross. Love did.

You'll give up on yourself before God will.

Know answered prayer when you see it, and don't give up when you don't.

Flattery is fancy dishonesty.

The right heart with the wrong creed is better than the right creed with the wrong heart.

We treat others as we perceive God is treating us.

Sometimes the most godly thing we can do is take a day off.

Faith in the future begets power in the past.

No one is useless to God. No one.

Conflict is inevitable. But combat is optional.

You will never forgive anyone more than God has already forgiven you.

Succeed in what matters.

You'll regret opening your mouth. You'll rarely regret keeping it shut.

To see sin without grace is despair. To see grace without sin is arrogance. To see them in tandem is conversion.

Faith is the grit in the soul that puts dare into dreams.

God doesn't keep a clock.

Never underestimate a gesture of affection.

When Jesus went home, he left the front door open.

And to sum it up:

As soon as you can, pay your debts.

As long as you can, give the benefit of the doubt.

As much as you can, give thanks. He's already given us more than we deserve.

SEEING WHAT THE EYES CAN'T

I stand six steps from the bed's edge. My arm's extended. Hands open. On the bed Luke—all four years of him—crouches, posed like a playful kitten. He's going to jump. But he's not ready. I'm too close. "Back more, Daddy," he stands and dares. I dramatically comply, confessing admiration for his courage. After two giant steps I stop. "More?" I ask. "Yes!" Luke squeals, hopping on the bed. With each step he laughs and claps, and motions for more. When I'm on the other side of the canyon, when I'm beyond the reach of mortal man, when I'm but a tiny figure on the horizon, he stops me. "There, stop there." "Are you sure?" "I'm sure," he shouts. I extend my arms. Once again he crouches, and then springs. Superman without a cape. Skydiver without a chute.

Only his heart flies higher than his body. In that airborne instant his only hope is his father. If he proves weak, he will fall. If he proves cruel, he will crash. If he proves forgetful, he will tumble to the hard floor.

But such fear he does not know, for his father he does. He trusts him. Four years under the same roof have convinced him he's reliable. He's not superhuman, but he is strong. He's not holy, but he is good. He's not brilliant, but he doesn't have to be to remember to catch his child when he jumps.

And so he flies.

And so he soars.

And so he catches him and the two rejoice at the wedding of his trust and his faithfulness.

I stand a few feet from another bed. This time no one laughs. The room is solemn. A machine pumps air into a tired body. Monitor metronomes the beats of a weary heart. The woman is no child. She was, once. Decades back. She was. But not now. Like Luke she must trust. Only days out of the operating room, she's just been told that she will have to return. Her frail hand squeezes mine. Her eyes mist with fear. Unlike Luke, she sees no father. But the father sees her. *Trust Him,* I say to us both. Trust the voice that whispers your name. Trust the hands to catch.

I sit across from the table of a good man. Good and afraid. His fear is honest. Stocks are down. Inflation is up. He has payroll to meet and bills to pay. He hasn't squandered or gambled or played. He has worked hard and prayed often, but now he is afraid. Beneath the flannel suit lies a timid heart.

He stirs his coffee and stares at me with the eyes of Wile E. Coyote who just realized that he has just ran beyond the edge of the cliff. He's about to fall and fall fast. He's Peter on the water, seeing the storm and not the face. He's Peter in the waves, hearing the wind and not the voice.

Trust, I urge. But the word thuds. He's unaccustomed to the strangeness. He's a man of reason. Even when the kite flies beyond the clouds he still holds the string. But now the string has slipped. And the sky is silent.

I stand a few feet from a mirror and see the face of a man who failed...who failed his Maker. Again. I promised I wouldn't, but I did. I was quiet when I should have been bold. I took a seat when I should have taken a stand. If this were the first time, it would be different. But it isn't. How many times can one fall and expect to be caught?

Trust. Why is it easier to tell others and so hard to remind self? Can God deal with death? I told the woman so. Can God deal with debt? I ventured as much as the man. Can God hear yet one more confession from these lips? The face in the mirror asks.

I sit a few feet from a man on death row. Jewish by birth. Tentmaker by trade. Apostle by calling. His days are marked. I'm curious about what bolsters this man as he nears his execution. So I ask some questions.

Do you have family, Paul? *I have none.* What about your health? *My body is beaten and tired.* What do you own? *I have my parchments. A pen. A cloak.* And your reputation? *Well, it's not much. I'm a heretic to some, a maverick to others.* Do you have any friends? *I do, but even some of them have turned their back.* Any awards? *Not on earth.* Then what do you have, Paul? No belongings. No family. Criticized by some. Mocked by others. What do you have, Paul? What do you have that matters?

I sit back quietly and watch. Paul rolls his hands into a fist. He looks at it. I look at it. What is he holding? What does he have? He extends his hands so I can see. As I lean forward, he opens his fingers. I peer at his palm. It's empty. *I have my faith. It's all I have. But it's all I need. I have kept the faith.*

Paul leans back against the wall of his cell and smiles. And I lean back against another and stare into the face of a man that has learned that there is more to life than meets the eye.

For that is what faith is. Faith is trusting what the eye can't see.

Eyes see prowling lions. Faith sees Daniel's angel.

Eyes see storms. Faith sees Noah's rainbow.

Eyes see giants. Faith sees Canaan.

Your eyes see your faults. Your faith sees your Savior.

Your eyes see your guilt. Your faith sees his blood.

Your eyes see your grave. Your faith sees a city whose builder and maker is God.

Your eyes look in the mirror and see a sinner, a failure, a promise-breaker. But by faith you look in the mirror and see a robed prodigal bearing the ring of grace on your finger and the kiss of your Father on you face.

But wait a minute, someone asks. How do I know that this is true? Nice prose, but give me the facts. How do I know these aren't just fanciful hopes?

Part of the answer can be found in Luke's little leaps of faith. His older sister, Juanita, was in the room watching, and I asked Luke if he would jump to Juanita. Luke refused. I tried to convince him. He wouldn't budge. "Why not?" I asked. "I only jump into big arms." If we think the arms are weak, we won't jump.

For that reason the Father flexes his muscles. "God's power is great for those who believe," Paul taught. "That power is the same as the great strength that God used to raise Christ from the dead." (Eph. 1:19-20)

Next time you wonder if God can catch you; read that verse. The very arms that defeated death are arms awaiting you. Next time you wonder if God can forgive you, read that verse. The very hands that were nailed to the cross are open for you. The next time you wonder if you will survive the jump, think of Luke and me. If a flesh-and-boneheaded dad like me can catch his child, don't you think your eternal Father can catch you?

THE CHOICE

"Why do I want to do bad?" my daughter asked me, unknowingly posing a question asked by many seekers of the truth. "Why do I do the thing I hate?" "if sin separates me from God, why doesn't God separate me from sin? Why doesn't he remove me from the option to sin?"

To answer that, let's go to the beginning. Let's go to the Garden and see the seed that both blessed and cursed. Let's see why God gave man…the choice.

Behind it all was a choice. A deliberate decision. An informed move. He didn't have to do it, but he chose to. He knew the price. He saw the implications. He was aware of the consequences.

We don't know when he decided to do it. We can't know. Not just because we weren't there, because time was not there. <u>When</u> did not exist. Nor did <u>tomorrow</u> or <u>yesterday</u> or <u>next time.</u> For there was no time.

We don't know when he thought about making the choice. But we do know that he made it. He didn't have to. He chose to.

He chose to create.

"In the beginning God created…"

With one decision, history began. Existence became measurable.

Out of nothing came light. Out of light came day. Then came the sky and the earth. And on this earth, a mighty hand went to work.

Canyons were carved. Oceans were dug. Mountains erupted out of flatlands. Stars were flung. A universe sparkled.

Our sun became just one of millions. Our galaxy became one of thousands. Planets invisibly tethered to the suns roar roared through space at breakneck speeds. Stars blazed with heat that could melt our planet in seconds.

The hand behind it was mighty. He is mighty. And with this might, he created. As naturally as birds sing and fish swim, he created. Just as an artist not paint, a runner not run, he couldn't not create. He was the creator. A tireless dreamer and designer.

Before there was a person to see it, his creation was pregnant with wonder. Flowers didn't just grow, they blossomed. Chicks weren't just born, they hatched.

He must have loved it. Creators relish creating. I'm sure his commands were delightful! "Hippo you won't walk… you'll waddle!" Giving the clouds their puff. Giving the oceans their blue. Giving the trees their sway. The mighty wed with the creative, and creation was born.

He was mighty. He was creative. And he was love. Even greater than his might and deeper that his creativity was one all-consuming characteristic:

Love.

Water must be wet. Fire must be hot. You can't take wet out of water nad still have water. You can't take heat out of fire and still have fire.

In the same sense you can't take the love out of this One who lived before time and still have him exist. For he was… and is…Love.

Probe deep within him. Explore every corner. Search every angle. Love is all you find. Go to the beginning of every decision he has made and you will find it. Go to the end of every story he has ever told and you'll see it.

Love.

No bitterness. No evil. No cruelty. Just love. Flawless love. Passionate love. Vast and pure love. He is love. The same God who was mighty enough to carve out the canyons is tender enough to put hair on the legs of a matter horn fly to keep him warm. The same force that provides symmetry to the planets guides a baby kangaroo to it's mothers pouch before she even knows it's born.

And because of who he was, he did what he did.

He created a paradise. A sinless sanctuary. A haven before. A home before there was a human dweller. No time. No death. No hurt. A gift built by God for his ultimate creation. And when he was through, he knew "it was very good."

But it wasn't enough.

His greatest work hadn't been completed. One final masterpiece was needed before he would stop.

Imagine with me what may have taken place that day.

He placed one scoop of clay upon another until a form lay lifeless on the ground.

All the Garden's inhabitants paused to witness the event.

"You will love me, nature." God said. "I made you that way. You will obey me, universe. For you were designed to do so. You will reflect my glory, skies for that is how you were created. But this one will be like me. This one will be able to choose."

All were silent as the Creator reached into himself and removed something yet to be seen. A seed. "it's called 'choice.' The seed of choice. Creation stood in silence and gazed upon a lifeless form.

An angel spoke, "but what if he…"

"What if he chooses not to love?" The creator finished. "Come, I will show you."

Unbound by today, God and the angel walked into the realm of tomorrow.

"There, see the fruit of the seed of choice, both sweet and the bitter."

The angel gasped at what he saw. Spontaneous love. Voluntary devotion. Chosen tenderness. Never has he seen anything like this. He felt the love of the Adams. He heard the joy of Eve and her daughters. He absorbed the kindness and marveled at the warmth.

"Ah, but you've only seen the sweet. Now witness the bitter."

A stench enveloped the pair. The angel turned in horror and proclaimed, What is it?"

The Creator only spoke one word: "Selfishness." Never have they seen such filth. Rotten hearts. Ruptured promises. Forgotten loyalties. Children of creation wandering blindly in lonely labyrinths.

"This is the result of choice?" the angel asked. "Yes" "They will forget you?" "Yes" They will reject you? "Yes"

"They will never come back?" "Some will. Most won't." "What will it take to make them listen?"

The Creator walked on in time, further and further into the future, until he stood by a tree. A tree that would be fashioned into a cradle.

With another step into the future, he paused before another tree. It stood alone, a stubborn ruler of a bald hill. The trunk was thick and the wood was strong. Soon it would be cut. Soon it would be trimmed. And soon he would be hung on it.

He felt the wood rub against his back he did not yet wear.

"Will you go down there?" the angel asked. "I will." "Is there any other way?" "There is not." "Wouldn't it be easier not to plant the seed? Wouldn't it be easier not to give the choice?" It would," the Creator spoke slowly. "But to remove the choice is to remove the love."

He looked around the hill and foresaw a scene. Three figures hung on three crosses. Arms spread. Heads fallen forward. They moaned with the wind.

All heaven stood to fight. All nature rose to rescue. But the creator gave no command.

"it must be done..," he said, and withdrew. But he stepped back in time, he heard the cry that he would someday scream: **"My God, my God, why have you forsaken me?"** He wrenched at tomorrows agony.

The angel spoke again. "it would be less painful..." The Creator interrupted softly. "But it wouldn't be love."

They stepped into the Garden again. The maker looked earnestly at the clay creation. A monsoon of love swelled up inside of him. He had died for the creation before he had made him. God's form bent over the sculptured face and breathed. Dust stirred on the lips of the new one. The chest rose, cracking the red mud. The cheeks fleshened. A finger moved. And an eye opened.

But more incredible than the moving of the flesh, was the stirring of the spirit. Those who could see the unseen gasped.

Perhaps it was the wind who said it first. Perhaps what the star saw is what made it blink ever since. Maybe it was left to an angel to whisper it:

"It looks like…it appears so much like…it is him!"

The angel wasn't speaking of the face, the features, or the body. He was looking inside-at the soul.

"It's eternal!" Gasped another.

Within the man, God has placed a divine seed. A seed of himself. The God of might had created the mightiest. The Creator had created, not a creature, but another creator. And the One who had chosen to love had created one who could love in return.

Now it's our choice.

THE GIFT OF UNHAPPINESS

There dwells inside of you, deep within, a tiny whippoorwill. Listen. You will hear him sing. His aria mourns the dusk. His solo signals the dawn.

It is the song of the whippoorwill.

He will not be silent until the sun is seen.

We forget he is there, so easy is he to ignore. Other animals of the heart are larger, noisier, more demanding, more imposing.

But none are so constant.

Other creatures of the soul are more quickly fed. More simply satisfied. We feed the lion who growls for power. We stroke the tiger who demands affection. We bridle the stallion who bucks control.

But what do we do with the whippoorwill who yearns for eternity?

For that is his song. That is his task. Out of the gray he sings a golden song. Perched in time he chirps a timeless verse. Peering through pain's shroud, he sees a painless place. Of that place he sings.

And though we try to ignore him, we cannot. He is us, and his song is ours. Our heart song won't be silent until we see the dawn.

"God has planted eternity in the hearts of men," says the wise man. But it doesn't take a wise person to know that people long for more than earth. When we see pain, we yearn. When we see hunger, we question why. Senseless deaths. Endless tears, needless loss. Where do they come from? Where will they lead?

Isn't there more to life than death?

And so sings the whippoorwill.

We try to quiet this terrible, tiny voice. Like a parent hushing a child, we place a finger over puckered lips and request silence. *I'm too busy now to talk. I'm too busy to think. I'm too busy to question.*

And we busy ourselves with the task of staying busy.

But occasionally we hear his song. And occasionally we let the song whisper to us that there is something more. There *must* be something different.

And as long as we hear the song, we are comforted. As long as we are discontent, we will search. As long as we know there is far-off country, we will hope.

The only ultimate disaster that can befall us, I have come to realize, is to feel ourselves to be at home on earth. As long as we are aliens, we cannot forget our true homeland.

Unhappiness on earth cultivates a hunger for heaven. By gracing us with deep dissatisfaction, God holds our attention. The only tragedy, then, is to be satisfied prematurely. To settle the earth. To be content in a strange land.

We are not happy here because we are not at home here. We are not happy here because we are not supposed to be happy here. We are "like foreigners and strangers in this world".

Take a fish and place him on the beach. Watch his gills gasp and scales dry. Is he happy? No! How do you make him happy? Do you cover him with a mountain of cash? Do you get him a beach chair and sunglasses? Do you bring him a *Playfish* magazine and a martini? Do you wardrobe him with a double-breasted fins and people-skinned shoes?

Of course not. The how do you make him happy? You put him back in his element. You put him back in the water. He will never be happy on the beach because he was not made for the beach.

And you will never be completely happy on earth simply because you were not made for earth. Oh, you will have your moments of joy. You will catch glimpses of light. You will know moments or even days of peace. But they simply do not compare with the happiness that lies ahead.

Thou has made us for thyself and our hearts are restless until they rest in thee.

Rest on this earth is false rest. Beware of those who urge you to find happiness here; you wont find it. Guard against the false physicians who promise that joy is only a diet away, a marriage away, or a transfer away.

Again, we have our moments. The newborn on our breast, the bride on our arm, the sunshine on our back. But even those moments are simply slivers of light breaking through heaven's window. God flirts with us. He tantalizes us. He romances us. Those moments are appetizers for the dish that is to come.

"No one has ever imagined what God has prepared for those that love Him."

What a breathtaking verse! Do you see what it says? *Heaven is beyond our imagination.* We cannot envision it. At our most creative moment, at our deepest thought, at our highest level, we still cannot fathom eternity.

Try this. Imagine a perfect world. Whatever that means to you, imagine it. Does that mean peace? Then envision absolute tranquility. Does that world imply joy? Then create your highest happiness. Will a perfect world have love? If so, ponder a place where love has no bounds. Whatever heaven means to you, imagine it. Get it firmly fixed in your mind. Delight in it. Dream about it. Long for it.

And then smile as the Father reminds you, *No one has ever imagined what God has prepared for those that love Him.*

Anything you imagine is inadequate. Anything anyone imagines is inadequate. No one has come close. No One.

It's beyond us.

But it's also within us. The song of the whippoorwill. Let her sing. Let her sing in the dark. Let her sing at the dawn. Let her song remind you that you were not made for this place and that there is a place made just for you.

But until then, be realistic. Lower your expectation of earth. This is not heaven, so don't expect it to be. There will never be a new car, new wife, or new baby who can give you the joy your heart craves. Only God can.

And God will. Be patient. And be listening. Listening for the song of the whippoorwill.

OVERCOMING YOUR INHERITANCE

Every generation must make a choice. They can either pillage or plant. They can rape the landscape and get rich; or they can care for the landscape; haven't only what is theirs; and leave an investment for their children.

We may harvest seeds sown by men we never knew. We are sowing seeds for descendant will never see.

Dependent on the past; responsible for the future. You're part of a choice. Children of the past; parents of the future. Heirs, benefactors, recipients of work done by those before. Born into a forest we didn't seed.

<u>Which leads me top ask, How is your Forest?</u> As you stand on the land bequeathed by your ancestors; how does it look? How do you feel?

Pride has legacy left? Maybe. Some nourished soil. Deeply rooted trees of conviction. Row after Row of truth and heritage. Could that be you. Give thanks cause many aren't.

Many aren't proud of their family trees. Poverty, shame, abuse. Such are the forest of some of you. The land is pillaged. Harvest was taken, but no seed sown.

Perhaps your childhood memories bring more hurt than inspiration. The voices of your past cursed you; belittled you;

even ignored you. At the time you thought such treatment was typical. Now you see it isn't. And now you try to explain your past.

I came across a man who must have had such thoughts. His heritage was tragic. Grandfather--murder, mystic, killed own children. Father—punk, ravaged house of worship, Mocked believers. He was killed at age 24 by his friends.

They were typical in their era. Prostitutes showed their goods in the houses of worship. People worshipped stars and followed horoscopes. More thought went into superstitions than education of the children.

What do you do when your grandfather is a murderer? Your father is a scoundrel and your nation is corrupt? You can hear the people moan "He is going to be just like his dad!"

They were Wrong!!!

He reversed the trend. He defiled the odds. He stood like a dam against the trend of his day, and enrooted the future of his nation.

It is the story of King Josiah. The world has seen wiser kings, wealthier kings, and more powerful kings. But history has never seen a more courageous king than Josiah. Born 600 years before Jesus, he inherited a fragile throne. Temple in disarray, the Law was lost. People worshipped whatever god they wanted. By the end of Josiah's 31 year reign; Temple rebuilt, idols destroyed, and the Law of God was once again elevated to a place of prominence and power. The forest has been reclaimed.

Josiah at 8 years old ascended the throne. Early in his reign Josiah made a brave choice. "He lived as his ancestor David lived, and he did not stop doing what was right."

He flipped through family scrapbook until he found an ancestor worthy of emulation. Skipped dad's life and bypassed grandpa's. Leaped back in time until he found David and resolved; "I'm going to be like him." The principle? We can't choose our parents, but we can choose our mentors.

And since Josiah chose David (who had chosen God); things began to happen.

Josiah wasn't out to make friends. He was out to make a statement. "What my fathers taught, I don't teach, what they embraced, I reject."

Four years later at age 26, he turned his attention to the temple. Josiah was determined. Something happened that fueled his passion to restore the temple. A baton had been passed. A torch had been received.

Early in his reign he resolved to serve the God of ancestor David. Now he chose to serve the God of someone else. (2 Chron. 34:8) In Josiah's 18 years as king, he made Judah and the Temple pure again. He sent Shaphan to repair the Temple of the Lord, The God of Josiah. (Personal) God was His God. David's faith was Josiah's faith. He had found the God of David and made him his own.

While the temple was being rebuilt, one of the workers found the scroll with the words that God had given Moses nearly 1000 years earlier. When he heard the words, he was shocked. He wept that his people had drifted so far away from God. He asked the prophetess, "What will become of our people?" She told Josiah since he had repented when he heard the words; his nation would be spared the anger of God. (2Chron. 34:27) Incredible!! An entire generation received grace because of the integrity of one man.

Could it be that God placed <u>him</u> in that place for that reason??

Could it be that God placed <u>You</u> on the earth for the same?

Maybe your past is not much to brag about. Maybe you've seen raw evil. <u>Now</u> you like Josiah, have to make a choice. Do you rise above the past and make a difference. Or do you remain controlled by the past and make excuses?

Many choose the comfortable homes of the heart. Healthy bodies; Sharp minds. But retired dreams. Back and forth they rock in a chair of regret, repeating the terms of surrender. Lean closely and you will hear them: (If Only." The white flag of the heart.

"If Only…" If only I'd been born somewhere else…"

"If Only I'd been treated fairly…"

"If Only I'd had kinder parents, more money, greater opportunity…"

Maybe you've used those words. Maybe you have every right to use them. Perhaps you, like Josiah you were hearing the 10 count before you got into the ring. Maybe for you to find an ancestor worth imitating, you'll have to look way back in the album.

If such is the case, let me show you where to turn. Put down your scrapbook and pick up your Bible. (John 3:6) "Human life comes from human parents, but spiritual life comes from the Spirit."

Think about that. Your parents may have given you genes, but God gives you grace. Your parents may be responsible for your body, but God has taken charge of your soul. You may get your looks from your mother, but you get eternity from your Father, your heavenly Father.

By the way, He's not blind to your problems. In fact, God is willing to give you what your family didn't.

-----Didn't have a good father? He'll be your Father.

(Gal 4:7) Through God you are a son; and if you are a son, then you are certainly an heir. Didn't have a good role model? Try God. (Eph. 5:1) You are God's children whom he loves, so try to be like him. Never had a parent to wipe away your tears? Think again. God has noted each one. (Psalm 56:8) You have seen me tossing and turning through the night. You have collected all my tears in your bottle. You have recorded everyone in your book"

God has not left you adrift on a sea of heredity. Just like Josiah, you can't control the way your fore-fathers responded to God, but you can control the way you respond to Him. The past doesn't have to be your prison. You have voice in your destiny. You have a say in your life. You have a choice in the path you take.

Choose well and someday—generations from now—your grandchildren and great-grandchildren will thank God for the seeds you sowed.

THE SWEET SONG OF THE SECOND FIDDLE

For thousands of years, their relationship had been perfect. As far back as anyone could remember, the moon had faithfully reflected the sun's rays into the dark night. It was the greatest duo in the universe. Other stars and planets marveled at the reliability of the team. Generations after generation of earthlings were captivated by the reflection. The moon became the symbol of romance, high hopes, and even nursery rhymes.

"Shine on, harvest moon," the people would sing. And he did. Well, in a way he did. You see, the moon didn't actually shine. He reflected. He took the light given to him by the sun and redirected it toward the earth. A simple task of receiving illumination and sharing it.

You would think such a combo would last forever. It almost did. But one day, a nearby star planted a thought in the moon's core. "It must be tough being the moon," the star suggested. "What do you mean? I love it! I've got an important job to do. When it gets dark, people look to me for help. And I look to the sun." "So you and the sun must be pretty tight." "Tight? Like peanut butter and jelly, Ren and

Stimpy, Jack and Diane…" "Or maybe like Edgar Bergen and Charlie McCarthy?" Who? "You know the man and the dummy." "Well I don't know about the dummy part." "That's exactly what I mean. You are the dummy. You don't have any light of your own. You depend on the sun. You're the sidekick. You don't have any name for yourself." "Name for myself?" "Yeah you've been playing second fiddle for too long. You need to step out on your own." "What do you mean?" "I mean stop reflecting and start generating. Do your own thing. Be your own boss. Get people to see you for who you really are." "Who am I?" "Well, you are, uh, well, uh, well, that's what you need to find out. You need to find out who you are." The moon paused and thought for a moment. What the star said made sense. Though he had never considered it, the moon was suddenly aware of all the inequities of the relationship.

Why should we have to work the night shift all the time? And why should he be the one the astronauts stepped on first? And why should he always be accused of making the waves? And why don't the dogs and the wolves howl at the sun for a change? And why should it be such an outrage to "moon" while "sunning is an accepted practice? "You are right!" Asserted the moon. "It's high time we had a solar-lunar equity up here." "Now you're taking," prodded the star. "Go discover the real moon!"

Such was the beginning of a breakup. Rather than turning his attention toward the sun, the moon began turning the attention toward himself.

He set out on a course of self-enhancement. After all, his complexion was a disgrace, so full of craters and all. His wardrobe was limited to three sizes; full-length, half-cast, and quarter-clad. And his color was an anemic yellow.

So, girded with determination, he set out to reach for the moon. He ordered glacier packs for his complexion. He changed his appearance to include new shapes such as triangular and square. And for color he opted for a punk-rock orange. "No one is going to call me cheese face anymore."

The new moon was slimmed down and shaped up. His surface was as smoothed as a baby's bottom. Everything was fine for a while. Initially, his new look left him basking at his own moonlight. Passing meteors would pause and visit. Distant stars would call and compliment. Fellow moons would invite him over to their orbits to watch "As the World Turns." He had friends. He had fame. He didn't need the sun-until the trends changed. Suddenly "punk" was out and "prep" was in. The compliments quit and the giggles began as the moon was slow to realize that he was out of style. Just as he finally caught on and had his orange changed to pinstripe, the style went to "country."

It was the painful poking of the rhinestones into his surface that caused him to finally ask himself, "What's this all for anyway? Are you on the cover of the magazine one day and forgotten the next. Living off the praise of others is an erratic diet." For the first time since he began his campaign to find himself, the moon thought of the sun. He remembered the good ol' millenniums when praise was not a concern. What people thought of him was immaterial since he wasn't in business of getting people to look at himself. Any praise that came his way was quickly passed on to the boss. The sun's plan was beginning to dawn on the moon. "He may have been doing me a favor." He looked down upon the earth. The earthlings have been getting quite a show. They never knew what to expect: first punk, then preppie, now country. Odds makers in Las Vegas were making bets as to whether the next style would be chic or macho. Rather than be the light of their world he was the butt of their jokes.

Even the cow refused to jump over him. But it was the cold that bothered him the most. Absence from the sunlight left him with a persistent chill. No warmth. No glow. His full-length overcoat didn't help. It couldn't help; the shiver was from the inside, an icy shiver from deep within his core that left him feeling cold and alone.

Which is exactly what he was.

One night as he looked down upon the people walking in the dark, he was struck by the futility of it all. He thought of the sun. *He gave me everything I needed. I served a purpose. I was warm. I was content. I was…I was what I was made to be.*

Suddenly, he felt the old familiar warmth. He turned and there was the sun. The sun had never moved. "I'm glad you're back," the sun said. "Let's get back to work. "You bet!" Agreed the moon. The coat came off. The roundness returned, and a light was seen in the dark sky. A light even fuller. A light even brighter. And to this day whenever the sun shines and the moon reflects and the darkness is illuminated, the moon doesn't complain or get jealous. He does what he was intended to do all along. The moon beams.

THE VOICE FROM THE MOP BUCKET

The hallway is silent except for the wheels of the mop bucket and the shuffle of the old mans feet. Both sounds tired. Both know these floors. How many nights has Hank cleaned them? He's always careful to get in the corners. He's always careful to set up his yellow caution sign warning of wet floors. Always chuckling as he does. "Be careful everyone," he laughs to himself, knowing no one is near. Not at three A.M.

Hank's health isn't what it used to be. Gout keeps him awake. Arthritis makes him limp. His glasses are so thick his eyeballs look twice their size. Shoulders stoop. But he does his work. Slopping soapy water on the floor. Scrubbing the heal marks left by the well-heeled lawyers. He'll be finished an hour before quitting time. Always finishes early. Has for twenty years.

When finished he'll put away his bucket and take a seat outside the office of the senior partner and wait. Never leaves early. Could. No one would ever know. But he doesn't. He broke the rules once, but never again.

Sometimes if the door is open, he'll enter the office. Not for long. Just to look. The suite is larger than his apartment. He'll run his fingers over the desk. He'll stroke the soft leather couch. He'll stand at the window and watch the gray sky turn gold. And he'll remember he once had an office.

Back when Hank was Henry. Back when the custodian was an executive. Long ago. Before the night shift. Before the mop bucket. Before the uniform. Before the scandal.

Hank doesn't think about it much now. No reason to. Got in trouble, got fired, got out. That's it. Not many people know about it. Better that way. No need to tell them. It's his secret.

Hank's story. The story is factual. You've heard it. You know it. When I give his real name you'll remember. But more than a true story, it's a common story. It's a story of a derailed dream. It's a story of high hopes colliding with harsh realities. Happens to all dreamers. And since all have dreamed, it's happened to us all. In Hank's case, it was a mistake he could never forget. A grave mistake. Hank killed someone. He came up on a thug beating on an innocent man, and Hank lost control. He killed the mugger. When word got out Hank got out.

Hank would rather hide than go to jail. So he ran. The executive became a fugitive. True story. Common story. Few spend their lives running from the law. Many, however, live with regrets. I could have gone to college, I could have done this or that, etc. But I joined a rock-n-roll band. Ended up never going. Now I'm stuck fixing garage doors. Now I'm stuck. Living a derailed dream. Pickup a high school yearbook and read the "What I want to do" sentence under each picture. You'll get dizzy breathing thin air of mountaintop visions. Yet take the yearbook to the twentieth-year reunion and read the next chapter. Some dreams have come true, but many haven't. Not that all should, mind you.

Changing direction is not tragic. Losing passion in life is. Something happens to us along the way. Convictions to change the world downgrade to commitment to pay the bills. Rather than make a difference we make a salary. Rather than look forward, we look back.. Rather than look outward we look inward. And we don't like what we see.

Hank didn't. Hank saw a man who settled for mediocre. Trained in the finest institutions of the world, yet working the night shift for minimum wage pay so he wouldn't be seen during the day. But all that changed when he heard a voice from the mop bucket.

At first he thought the voice was a joke. Some of the guys on the tird floor play these kind of tricks. "Henry, Henry," the voice called. Hank turned. No one called him Henry anymore. "Henry, Henry." He turned toward the pail. It was glowing. Bright red. Hot red. He could feel the heat ten feet away. He stepped closer and looked in. The water wasn't boiling. "This is strange," Henry mumbled to himself as he took another step to get a closer look. But the voice stopped him. "Don't come any closer. Take off your shoes you are on holy tile." Suddenly Hank knew who was speaking. "God?"

Sounds crazy almost irreverent. God speaking from a hot mop bucket to a janitor named Hank? Would it be believable if I said God was speaking from a burning bush to a shepherd named Moses? Maybe that one's easier to handle—because you've heard it before. But just because it's Moses and a bush rather than Hank and a bucket, it's no less spectacular.

It sure knocked the sandals off of Moses. We wonder what amazed the old fellow more: that God spoke in a bush or that he spoke at all.

Moses like Hank had made a mistake.

You remember his story. Adopted nobility. An Israelite reared in an Egyptian palace. His countrymen were slaves, but Moses was privileged. Ate at the royal table. Educated in the finest schools. But his most influential teacher had no degree. She was his mother. A Jewess who was hired to be his nanny. "Moses," you can almost hear her whisper to her young son, "God has put you here on purpose. Someday you will set your people free. Never forget, Moses. Never forget."

Moses didn't. The flame of justice grew hotter until it blazed. Moses saw an Egyptian beating a Hebrew slave. Just like Hank killed the mugger, Moses killed the Egyptian. The next day Moses saw the Hebrew. You'd think the slave would say thanks. He didn't. Rather than express gratitude, he expressed anger. "Will you kill me too?" he asked. (Exodus 2:14)

Moses knew he was in trouble. He fled Egypt and hid in the wilderness. Call it a career shift. He went from dining with the heads of state to counting heads of sheep. Hardly an upward move. And so it happened that a bright, promising Hebrew began herding sheep in the hills. From the Ivy League to the cotton patch. From an Oval office to a taxicab. From swinging a golf club to digging a ditch.

Moses thought the move was permanent. There is no indication that he ever intended to go back to Egypt. In fact, there is every indication that he wanted to stay with his sheep. Standing barefoot before the bush, he confessed,

"I am not a great man! How can I go to the king and lead the Israelites out of Egypt?" (Exodus 3:11)

I'm glad Moses asked that question. It's a good one. Why Moses? Or, more specifically, why eighty-year-old Moses? The forty-year-old was more appealing. The Moses we saw in Egypt was brash and confident. But the Moses we see four decades later is reluctant and weather-beaten. Had you or I looked at Moses back in Egypt, we would have said, "This man is ready for battle." Educated in the finest system of the world. Trained by the ablest soldiers. Instant access to the inner circle of the Pharaoh. Moses spoke their language and knew their habits. He was the perfect man for the job. Moses at forty we like. But Moses at eighty? No way. Too old. Too tired. Smells like a shepherd. Speaks like a foreigner. What impact would he have on Pharaoh? He's the wrong man for the job.

And Moses would have agreed. "Tried that once," he would say. Those people don't want to be helped. Just leave me here to tend to my sheep. They're easier to lead." Moses wouldn't have gone. You wouldn't have sent him.

But God did. How do you figure? Benched at forty and suited up at eighty. Why? What does he know now that he didn't know then? What did he learn in the desert that he didn't learn in Egypt? The way of the desert, for one. Forty-year-old Moses was a city boy. Now Moses knows the name of every snake and location of every water hole. If he's going to lead thousands of Hebrews into the wilderness, he better know the basics of desert life.

Family dynamics, for another. If He's going to be traveling with families for forty years, it might help to understand how they work. He marries a woman of faith, the daughter of a Medianite priest, and establishes his own family.

But more than the ways of the desert and the people, Moses needs to learn something about himself. Apparently he has learned it. God says Moses is ready. And to convince him, God speaks through a bush.(Had to do something dramatic to get Moses' attention.)

"School's out," God tells him. "Now it's time to get to work." Poor Moses. He didn't even know he was enrolled. But he was. And, guess what. So are you. The voice from the bush is the voice that whispers to you. It is the voice that reminds you that God is not finished with you yet. Oh, you may think he is. You may think you have peaked. You may think he has got someone else to do the job.

If so, think again.

"God began doing a good work in you, and I am sure he will continue it until it is finished when Jesus Christ comes again."

Did you see what God is doing? A good work in you.

Did you see when he will be finished? When Jesus comes again.

May I spell out the message? God ain't finished with you yet.

Your father wants you to know that. And to convince you, he may surprise you. He may speak through a bush, a mop bucket, or stranger still, he may speak through me.

WHAT IS YOUR PRICE?

Attending a game show wasn't your idea of a vacation activity, but your kids wanted to go, so you gave in. Now that you are here, you are beginning to enjoy it. The studio frenzy is contagious. The music is upbeat. The stage is colorful. And the stakes are high.

"Higher than they have ever been!" The show host brags. "Welcome to *What Is Your Price?*" You're just about to ask your wife if that is his real hair when he announces the pot: "Ten million dollars!"

The audience needs no prompting; they explode with applause.

"It's the richest game in history," the host beams. "Someone here today will walk out of here with a check for ten million!"

"Won't be me," you chuckle to your oldest child. "I've never had any luck at luck."

"Shhhh," she whispers, pointing to the stage. "They are about to draw the name."

Guess whose name they call. In the instant it takes to call it, you go from spectator to player. Your kids shriek, your spouse screams, and a thousand eyes watch the pretty girl take your hand and walk you to the stage.

"Open the curtain!" the host commands. You turn and watch as the curtains part and you gasp at the sight. A bright wheel barrel full of money—overflowing with money. The same girl who walked you over to the stage now pushes the wheel barrel in your direction, parking it right in front of you.

"Ever seen ten million dollars?" asks the pearly teeth host.

"Not in a while," you answer. The audience laughs like you were a stand-up comic.

"Dig your hands in it," he invites. "Go ahead, dive in."

You look at your family. One child is drooling, the other is praying, and your mate is giving you two thumbs up. How can you refuse? You burrow up in to your shoulders and rise up, clutching up a chestful of one-hundred dollar bills.

"It can be yours. It can all be yours. The choice is up to you. The only question you have to answer is, 'What is your price?'"

Applause ring again, the band plays, and you swallow hard. Behind you a second curtain opens, revealing a large placard. "What are you willing to give?" is written on the top. The host explains the rules. "All you have to do is agree to one condition and you will receive the money."

"Ten million dollars!" you whisper to yourself.

Not one million or two, but *ten* million. No small sum. Nice nest egg. Ten million bucks would go a long way, right? Tuition paid off. Retirement guaranteed. Would open a few doors on a few cars or a new house (or several).

You could be quite the benefactor with such a sum. Help a few orphanages. Feed a few nations. Build some church buildings. Suddenly you understand: This is the opportunity of a lifetime.

"Take your pick. Just choose one option and the money is yours."

A deep voice from another microphone begins reading the list.

"Put your children up for adoption."

"Become a prostitute for a week."

"Give up your American citizenship."

"Abandon your church."

"Kill a stranger."

"Have sex-change operation."

"Leave your spouse."

"Change your race."

"That's the list," the host proclaims. "Now make your choice."

The theme music begins, the audience is quiet, and your pulse is racing. You have a choice to make. No one can help you. The decision is yours. No one can tell you what to pick.

But there is one thing I can tell you, I can tell you what others will do. Your neighbors would have given their answers. In a national survey that asked the same question, many said what they would do. Seven percent said they would kill for money. Six percent would change their race. Four percent would change their sex.

If money is the gauge of the heart, then this study revealed that money is on the heart of most Americans. In exchange for ten million dollars:

25 percent would abandon their families.

25 percent would abandon their church.

23 percent would become a prostitute for a week.

16 percent would give up their American citizenship.

16 percent would leave their spouse.

3 percent would put up their children for adoption.

Even more revealing what Americans would do for ten million dollars is that most would do *something*. Two-third of those polled would agree to at least one-some to several-of the options. The majority, in other words, would not leave the stage empty-handed. They would pay the price to own the wheelbarrow.

What would you do? Or better, what are you doing?

"Get real Mike," you are saying. "I've never had a shot at ten million."

Perhaps not, but you have had a chance to make a thousand or a hundred, or ten. The amount may not have been the same, but the choices are. Some are willing to give up their families, faith, or morals for far less than ten million dollars.

Jesus had a word for that: *greed*.

Jesus also had a definition for greed. He called it the practice of measuring life by possessions.

Greed equates to a person's worth with a person's purse.

1. You got a lot = you are a lot.
2. You got a little = you are little.

If you are the sum of what you own, then by all means own it all. No price too high. No payment too much. Greed is not defined by what something cost; it is measured by what it cost you.

If anything cost you your faith or your family, the price is too high.

Such is the point Jesus makes in the parable of the portfolio. Seems a fellow made a windfall profit off an investment. He found himself with excess cash and an enviable question, "What will I do with my earnings?"

Doesn't take him long to decide. He will save it. He will find a way to store it so he can live the good life. His plan? Accumulate. His aim? Wine, dine, shine, and recline. Move to the Sunbelt, play golf, kick back, and relax.

Suddenly, the man dies and another voice is heard. The voice of God. God has nothing kind to say to the man. His initial words are "Foolish man!"

On the earth the man was respected. He is honored with a nice funeral and a mahogany casket. Gray flannels fill the auditorium with admiration for the canny businessman. But on the front pew is a family already starting to biker over their dad's estate. "Foolish man!" God declares. "So who will get those things you have prepared for yourself?"

The man spent his life building a house of cards. He never saw the storm. And now, the wind has blown.

The storm wasn't the only thing he didn't see.

He never saw God. Note the first words after the capital gain. *"What will I do?"* he went to the wrong place and asked the wrong question. What if he had gone to God and asked, "What will you have me do?"

The man's sin was not that he planned for the future, but that he did not include God.

Imagine if someone had treated you like this. Let's say you bring over a house sitter to care for your home over a weekend. You leave her with keys, money, and instructions. And you leave to enjoy your trip.

When you return, you find that your house has been painted purple. The locks have been changed, so you ring the doorbell and the house sitter answers. Before you can say anything, she escorts you proclaiming, "Look how I decorated my house!"

The fireplace has been replaced with an indoor waterfall. Carpet has been replaced with pink tile, and portraits of Elvis on black velvet line the walls.

"This isn't your house!" you proclaim. "It's mine!"

"Those aren't your possessions," God reminds us. "They are mine."

"The Lord owns the world and everything in it—the heavens, even the highest heavens, are his." God's foremost rule of finance is: We own nothing. We are managers, not owners. Stewards, not landlords. Maintenance people, not proprietors. Our money is not ours, it is his.

This man, however, gave no thought to that. Please note that Jesus did not criticize this man's affluence. He criticized his arrogance. The rich ma's words testify to his priority.

This is what I will do:
I will tear down...
I will store...
Then I can say to myself, "I will have enough good things."

A school boy was once asked to define the parts of speech, *I* and *mine*. He answered, "Aggressive pronouns." This man was aggressively self-centered. His world was fenced in by himself. He was blind. He didn't see God. He didn't see others. He only saw self.

"Foolish man," God told him. "Tonight your life will be taken from you."

Strange, isn't it, this man had enough sense to acquire wealth, but not enough to get ready for eternity? Stranger still, that we make the same mistake. I mean, it's not like God kept the future a secret. One glance at a cemetery should remind us; everyone dies. One visit to a funeral should convince us; we don't take anything with us.

Hearses pull no U—Hauls.

Dead men push no ten—million—dollar wheelbarrows. The game show was pretend, but the facts are real. You are on a stage. You have been given a prize. The stakes are high. Very High. What is your price?

YOUR SACK OF STONES

You have one. A Sack. Probably aren't aware of it, may not have been told about it. Could be you don't remember it. But it was given to you. A sack. An itchy scratchy sack.

You needed the sack so you could carry the stones. Rocks, boulders, pebbles, all sizes, shapes, and all of them unwanted.

You don't request them. You didn't seek them. But you were given them. Don't remember?

Some were rocks of rejection. You were given one when you didn't make the tryouts. It wasn't for lack of effort. Heaven only knows how hard you practiced. You thought you were good enough for the team. But the coach didn't. The instructor didn't. You thought you were, but they said you weren't. They and how many others?

You didn't have to live long before you get a collection of stones. Make a poor grade. Make a bad choice. Make a mess. Get called a few names. Get mocked. Get abused.

So the sack gets heavy. Heavy with stones. Stones we don't deserve. Along with a few we do.

Look into your sack and you see that not all the stones are from rejection. There is a 2nd type of stone. The stone of regret.

- Regret for the time you lost your temper
- "   " day you lost control
- "   " moment you lost your pride
- "   " years you lost your priorities

One stone after another, one guilty stone after another. With time the sack gets

Heavy. We get tired. How can you have dreams for the future when all your energy is required is to shoulder the past?

No wonder so many people look miserable. The sack slows the steps. The sack chafes. Helps explain the irritation on so many faces, the sag in so many steps, the drag in so many shoulders, and most of all the desperation in so many acts.

You're consumed with doing whatever it takes to get some rest. So you take the sack to school, work. You resolve to work so hard you forget about the sack. You arrive early and stay late. People are impressed. But when it is time to go home, there is a sack—waiting to be carried out.

You carry the sack to the hang out. You set the sack on the floor, sit in the couch, maybe you'll drink, smoke, something. The music gets loud and your head gets light. But then it's time to go and look down and there is the sack.

You drag it to your friends. Throw yourself on the couch with the sack at your feet and spill all your stones on the floor and name them one by one. Your friend listens she empathizes. Some helpful counsel is given, but when time is up your obligated to gather all your stones and take them with you.

Some even take the sack to church. Perhaps religion will help, we reason. But instead of removing a few stones, some well—meaning but misguided person may add to the load. God's messengers sometimes give more hurt than help. You may leave the church with a few new rocks in your sack.

The result? A person slugging his way through life, weighed down by the past. I don't know if you have noticed, but it's hard to be thoughtful when you are carrying an emotional sack. It is hard to be affirming when you're affirmation—starved. It's hard to be forgiving when you feel guilty.

Paul had an interesting observation about the way we treat people. He said it about marriage, but the principle applies to any relationship. "The man who loves his wife loves himself". (EPH. 5:28). There is a correlation between the way you feel about yourself and the way you feel about others. If you are at peace with yourself—if you like yourself—you will get along with others.

The converse is also true. If you don't like yourself—if you're ashamed, embarrassed, or angry, other people are going to know it. The tragic thing about the story of our sack is that we tend to throw our stones at those we love.

Unless the cycle is interrupted. This takes us to the question, "How does the person get relief??"

Which in turn, takes us to one of the kindest verses in the Bible; "Come to meet all who are tired with heavy loads, and I will give you rest. Accept my teachings, and learn from me, because I am gentle and humble in spirit, and you will find rest in your lives. The teaching I ask for you to accept is easy; the load I will give to you is light to carry. (Matt. 11:28-29)".

You are probably saying, "I've tried that. I've read the Bible. I've sat on the pew—but I've never received relief."

If that is the case; could I ask a delicate but deliberate question? Could it be that you went to religion and not to God? Could it be that you went to church but never saw Christ?

"Come to me" the verse reads. It easy to go to the wrong place. It's not that you haven't tried—you've tried for years to deal with your past. Drugs, sex, religion, or manipulation.

Jesus says he's the solution for weariness of the soul. Go to him be honest with him. Admit you have soul secrets that you've never dealt with. He already knows what they are. He's just waiting for you to ask him to help. He's just waiting for you to give him your sack. Go ahead you'll be glad you did. (Those near to you will be glad as well) it's hard to throw the stones when you've left the sack at the cross.

YOU MIGHT'VE BEEN IN THE BIBLE

There are a few stories in the Bible where everything turns out right. This is one. It has three characters.

The first is Philip----a disciple in the early church who had a penchant for lost people. One day he was instructed by God to go to the road that leads to Gaza from Jerusalem. It was a desert road. He went. When he arrived he came upon a ruler from Ethiopia.

Must have been a bit intimidating for Philip. It would be similar to your hopping on a motor scooter and following the secretary of the treasury. At the stoplight you notice he is reading the Bible, and you volunteer your services.

That is what Philip did.

"Do you understand what you are reading?"

"How can I unless someone explains it to me?"

And so Philip did. They have a Bible study in the chariot. The study is so convicting that the Ethiopian is baptized that day. And then they separate. Philip goes one way and the Ethiopian goes another. The story has a happy ending. Philip teaches, the Ethiopian obeys, and the gospel is sent to Africa.

But that's not all the story. Remember I said there were three characters. The first was Philip: the second was the

Ethiopian. Did you see the third? There is one. Read these verses and take note.

"An angel of the Lord said to Philip, 'Get ready and go south....' So Philip got ready and went" **(Acts 8:26-27)**

"The Spirit said to Philip, 'Go to that chariot and stay near it.' So...Philip ran toward the chariot" **(Acts 8:29-30)**.

The third character? God! God sent the angel. The Holy Spirit instructed Philip; God orchestrated the entire moment! He saw this godly man coming from Ethiopia to worship. He saw his confusion. So he decided to resolve it.

He looked in Jerusalem for a man he could send. He found Philip.

Our typical response when we read these verses is to think Philip was a special guy. He had access to the Oval Office. He carried his first-century pager that God doesn't pass out anymore.

But don't be too quick. In a letter to Christians just like us, Paul wrote, "Live by following the Spirit" **(gal. 5:16)**

"The true children of God are those who let God's Spirit lead them" **(Rom. 8:14)**

To hear many of us talk, you'd think we didn't believe these verses. You'd think we didn't believe in the Trinity. We talk about the Father and study the Son---but when it comes to the Holy Spirit, we are confused at best and frightened at worse. Confused because we have never been taught. Frightened because we've been taught to be afraid.

May I simplify things a bit? The Holy Spirit is the presence of God in our lives, carrying on the work of Jesus. The Holy Spirit helps us in three directions—inwardly (by granting us fruits of the spirit, **Gal. 5:22-24**), upwardly (by praying for us, **Rom. 8:26**) and outwardly (by pouring God's love into our hearts, **Rom. 5:5**).

In evangelism the Holy Spirit is on center stage. If the disciple teaches, it is because the Spirit teaches the disciple (**Luke 12:12**). If the listener is convicted, it is because the Spirit has penetrated (**16:10**). If the listener is converted, it is by the transforming Power of the Spirit (**Rom 8:11**). If the new believer matures, it is because the Spirit makes him or her competent (**2 Cor. 3:6**).

You have the same Spirit working with you that Philip did. Some of you don't believe me. You are still cautious. I can hear you mumbling under your breath as you read, "Philip had something I don't. I've never heard an angel's voice." To which I counter, "How do you know Philip did?"

We assume he did. We've been taught he did. The flannelboard figures say he did. An angel puts his trumpet in Philip's ear, blares the announcement, and Philip has no choice. Flashing lights and fluttering wings are nothing to deny. The deacon had to go. But could our assumption be wrong? Could it be that the angel's voice was every bit as miraculous as the one you and I hear?

What?

You've heard the voice whispering your name, haven't you? You've felt the nudge to go and sensed the urge to speak. Hasn't it occurred to you?

You invite a couple over for coffee. Nothing heroic, just a nice evening with old friends. But from the moment they enter, you can feel the tension. Colder than glaciers, they are. You can tell something is wrong. Typically you are not one to inquire, but you feel a concern that won't be silent. So you ask.

You are in a business meeting where one of your coworkers gets raked over the coals. Everyone else is thinking, I'm glad that wasn't me. But the Holy Spirit is leading you to think, How hard this must be. So, after the meeting you approach the employee and express your concern.

You notice the fellow on the other side of the church auditorium. He looks a bit out of place, what with his strange clothing and all. You learn he is from Africa, in town on business. The next Sunday he is back. And the third Sunday he is present. You introduce yourself. He tells you how he is fascinated by the faith and how he wants to learn more. Rather than offer to teach him, you simply urge him to read the Bible.

Later in the week, you regret not being more direct. You call the office where he is consulting and learn that he is leaving today for home. You know in your heart that you can't let him leave. So you rush to the airport and find him waiting his flight, with a Bible open in his lap.

"Do you understand what you are reading?" You inquire.

"How can I unless someone explains it to me?"

And so you, like Philip, explain. And he, like the Ethiopian, believes. Baptism is requested and baptism is offered. He catches a later flight and you catch a glimpse of what it is to be led by the Spirit.

Were there lights? You just lit one. Were there voices? You just were one. Was there a miracle? You just witnessed one. Who knows? If the Bible were being written today, that might be your name in the eighth chapter of Acts.

THE GOD WHO FIGHTS FOR YOU

Here is the big question. What is God doing when you are in a bind? When the lifeboat springs a leak? When the life cord snaps? When the last penny is gone before the last bill is paid? When the last hope was left on the last train. What is God doing?

I know what we are doing. Nibbling on nails like corn on the cob. Pacing floors. Taking pills. I know what we do.

But what does God do? Big question. Real Big. If God is sleeping, I'm duck soup. If he is laughing, I'm lost. If he is crossing his arms and shaking his head, then saw off the limb, Honey, it's time to crash.

What is God doing?

Well, I decided to research that question. Being the astute researcher that I am, I discovered some ancient writings that may answer this question. Few people are aware—in fact, no one is aware—that newspaper journalist roamed the lands of the Old Testament era.

Yes, it is true that in the days of Noah, Abraham, and Moses, reporters were fast on the scene recording the drama of their days. And now, for the first time, their articles are going to be shared.

How did I come upon them? One might ask.

Well, I discovered them pressed between the pages of many books of the word of God. Ancient newspaper interviews with Moses and Jehoshaphat. I proudly share with you heretofore undiscovered conversations with two men who will answer the question: What does God do when we are in a bind?

The first interview is between the *Holy Land Press* (HLP) and Moses.

HLP: Tell us about your conflict with the Egyptians.

Moses: Oh, the Egyptians—big people. Strong fighters. Mean as snakes.

HLP: But you got away.

Moses: Not before they got washed away.

HLP: You're talking about the Red Sea conflict.

Moses: You're right. That was scary.

HLP: Tell us what happened.

Moses: Well, the Red Sea was on one side and the Egyptians were on the other.

HLP: So you attacked?

Moses: Are you kidding? With a half-a-million rock stackers? No, my people were too afraid. They wanted to go back to Egypt.

HLP: So you told everyone to retreat?

Moses: Where? Into the water? We didn't have a boat. We didn't have anywhere to go.

HLP: What did your leaders recommend?

Moses: I didn't ask them. There wasn't time.

HLP: Then what did you do?

Moses: I told the people to stand still.

HLP: You mean, with the enemy coming, you told them not to move?

Moses: Yep. I told the people, "Stand still and you will see the Lord save you."

HLP: Why would you want the people to stand still?

Moses: To get out of God's way. If you don't know what to do, it's best to just sit tight till he does his thing.

HLP: That's an odd strategy, don't you think?

Moses: It is if you're big enough for the battle. But when the battle is bigger than you are and you want God to take over, it's all you can do.

HLP: Can we talk about something else?

Moses: It's your paper.

HLP: Soon after your escape…

Moses: Our deliverance.

HLP: What's the difference?

Moses: There is a big difference. When you escape, *you* do it. When you are delivered, someone else does it and you just follow.

HLP: Okay, soon after your deliverance, you battled with the Ammo…Amala… let's see, I have it here…

Moses: The Amalekites.

HLP: Yeah, the Amalekites.

Moses: Big people. Strong fighters. Mean as snakes.

HLP: But you won.

Moses: God won.

HLP: Okay—God won—but you did the work. You fought the battle. You were on the field.

Moses: Wrong.

HLP: What? You weren't in the battle?

Moses: Not that one. While the army was fighting, I took my friends Aaron and Hur to the top of the hill and we did our fighting up there.

HLP: With each other?

Moses: With the darkness.

HLP: With swords?

Moses: No, in prayer. I lifted my hands to God, like I did at the Red Sea, only this time I forgot my rod. When I lifted my hands we would win, but when I would lower my arms we would lose. So I got my friends to hold up my arms until the Amalekites were history and we won.

HLP: Hold on a second. You think that standing on that hill with your hands in the air made a difference?

Moses: You don't see any Amalekites around, do you?

HLP: Don't you think that the general if the army stays on the mountain and the soldiers fight in the valley?

Moses: If the battle had been in the valley I would have gone, but that's not where the battle was being fought.

HLP: Odd, this strategy of yours.

Moses: You mean if your father was bigger than the fellow beating you up, you wouldn't call his name?

HLP: What?

Moses: If some guy has you on the ground and is pounding on you and your father is within earshot and tells you to call him anytime you need help what would you do?

HLP: I'd call my father.

Moses: That's all I do. When the battle is too great, I ask God to take over. I get the father to fight for me.

HLP: And he comes?

Moses: Seen any Jews building pyramids lately?

HLP: Let me see if I've got this straight. Once you defeat the enemy by standing still and another time you win by holding up your hands. Where did you pick all this up?

Moses: Well, if I told you, you wouldn't believe me.

HLP: Try me.

Moses: Well, you see, there was this bush on fire and it spoke to me...

Maybe you're right. We'll save that one for another day.

The second interview moves us ahead in history a couple of centuries. Here is King Jehoshaphat (KJ) in postwar interview with the *Jerusalem Chronicle* (JC) on the battlefield of Ziz.

JC: Congratulations, King.

KJ: For What?

JC: You just defeated three armies at on time. You defeated the Moabites, Ammonites, and Meunites.

KJ: Oh, I didn't do that.

JC: Don't be so modest. Tell us what you think of these armies.

KJ: Big people. Strong fighters. Mean as snakes.

JC: How did you feel when you heard they were coming?

KJ: I was scared.

JC: But you handled it pretty calmly. That strategy session with you generals must have paid off.

KJ: We didn't have one.

JC: You didn't have a meeting or you didn't have a strategy?

KJ: Neither>

JC: What did you do?

KJ: I asked God what to do.

JC: What did he say?

KJ: Nothing at first, so I got some people to talk to him with me.

JC: Your cabinet had a prayer session?

KJ: No, my nation went on a fast.

JC: The Whole nation?

KJ: Everyone but you, apparently.

JC: Uh, well, what did you tell God?

KJ: Well, we told God that he was king and whatever he wanted was ok with us, but if he wouldn't mind, we'd like his help on a big problem.

JC: *Then* you had your strategy session.

KJ: No.

JC: What did you do?

KJ: We stood before God.

JC: Who did?

KJ: All of us. The men. The women. The babies. We just stood there and waited.

JC: What was the enemy doing while you were waiting?

KJ: They were getting closer.

JC: Is that when you rallied the people?

KJ: Who told you I rallied the people?

JC: Well, I just assumed…

KJ: I never said anything to the people. I just listened. After a while this young fellow named Jahaziel spoke up and said the Lord said not to be discouraged or afraid because the battle wasn't ours, but it was his.

JC: How did you know he was speaking for God?

KJ: When you spend enough time speaking with God as I do, you learn to recognize his voice.

JC: Incredible.

KJ: No, supernatural.

JC: Then you attacked?

KJ: No, Jahaziel said, "Stand still and you will see the Lord save you."

JC: I've heard that somewhere.

KJ: Vintage Moses.

JC: Then you attacked?

KJ: No, then we sang. Well, someone sang. I'm not much with a tune so I fell on my face and prayed. I let the others sing. We've got this group—Levites—who really know how to sing.

JC: Wait a minute. With the army getting closer, you sang?

KJ: A few tunes. Then I told the people to be strong and have faith in God and then we marched onto the battlefield.

JC: And you led the army?

KJ: No, we put the singers out in front. And as we marched they sang. God set ambushes. And by the time we got to the battlefield, the enemy was dead. That was three days ago. It took us that long to clean up the area. We are back today to have a worship service. Come over here; I want you to listen to the Levites sing. I bet you ten shekels you can't keep your seat for five minutes.

JC: Wait. I can't write this story. It's too bizarre. Who'll believe it?

KJ: Just write it. Those with man-size problems will laugh. And those with God-size problems will pray. Leave it to them to decide. Come on. The band is tuning up. You won't want to miss this first piece.

So, what do you think? What does God do when we are in a bind? If Moses and Jehoshaphat are any indication, that question can be answered with one word: *fights*. He fights for us. He steps into the ring and points us to our corner and takes over. "Remain calm; the Lord will fight for you" (Exod. 14:14).

His job is to fight. Our job is to trust.

Just trust. Not direct. Or question. Or yank the steering wheel out of his hands. Our job is to wait and pray. Nothing more is necessary. Nothing more is needed.

"He is my defender; I will not be defeated" (Ps. 62:6). By the way, was it just me, or did I detect a few giggles when I discovered my archaeological discovery?

Some of you didn't believe me, did you? Tsk, tsk, tsk… Just for that you are going to have to wait until the next book before I tell you about the diary of Jonah I found in a used-book store in Texico, New Mexico. Still has some whale guts in it.

And you thought I was kidding.

I DID WHAT YOU JUST DID. I just read this book. So I sat in my office with a cup of coffee, and highlighter and sipped and read and...gratefully...smiled.

I liked it. You might find that surprising. You might assume that every writer likes what he or she writes. They should and normally do, I suppose. But I always have that lingering fear that with all the work done, I might sit down to read what I wrote...and gag.

But, I didn't. I was pleased.

I smiled at the right spots and was warmed at others. It was good to visit the seashore again and see the Master touching the people.

It was good to be reminded again that this journey is a brief one. That Jesus knows how I feel and that he'd scramble off a mountain and walk through a storm to remind me of that.

It was good to hear God's gentle thunder. I hope it has been good for you. Thanks for reading my book. I realize that it took your time. I hope that it has been worth it.

And I hope you never forget the Lighthouse Law. Approach life like a voyage on a schooner. Enjoy the view. Explore the vessel. Make friends with the captain. Fish a little. And then get off when you get home.

Good sailing!

ABOUT THE AUTHOR

Michael was born in a small town in Texas. He was raised with his two sisters and three brothers by their single mother. He is a member of Journey Church in Jacksonville, Florida. Michael has a lovely wife, Maryjane, and together they have six children. Being part of a blended family, Michael has been able to look at some of the most difficult situations and been able to see the silver lining in the situations that many of us may be in.

Printed in the United States
By Bookmasters